Bighead

by

Vince Cross

Illustrated by Pulsar Studios

For Robin Boult: top man and great guitar player.

With special thanks to:
Rebecca Brandt
Jake Cam
Yasmin Ewers
George Howlett
Harry Leighfield
William Mullins
Louise Norris
Sarah Norris
Kirsty Tracey

First published in 2011 in Great Britain by
Barrington Stoke Ltd
18 Walker St, Edinburgh, EH3 7LP

www.barringtonstoke.co.uk

ISBN: 978-1-84299-829-8

Printed in China by Leo

Contents

Chapter 1
The Wheelchair

It was going to snow. The TV weather girl said so. Andy's mum, Sue, picked up her car keys. Then put them down. Then picked them up again.

"Oh, Mum!" said Andy, spinning his wheelchair round on the wooden floor of the sitting room, "Go and dance. You know you want to."

"I hate driving when there's ice on the roads," Sue said, checking her make-up in the hall mirror.

"You'll be fine," Andy said. "Anyway, you might meet someone nice at Salsa ..."

"Andrew! You know that's not why I go. You just want me out of the way so you can scare the mice with your guitar playing."

"Daz's gonna come round later to play the piano. Is that OK?" Andy asked as if it.

"I suppose so. Just keep the noise down ..."

"Tess might come too."

"And?"

"Maybe Matt and his snare drum ..."

Andy's mum didn't mind. She was a secret rock chick. There was a pair of black leather trousers in her wardrobe. And she loved her Motörhead T-shirts.

Until the car smash which left Andy in a wheelchair, and until his dad had walked out, Sue had always sung in clubs. These days she thought her singing days were over.

While Sue was out bopping, the four of them jammed. Then they stopped for a drink and a chat.

"The thing is," said Daz, "We were thinking of forming a band. A proper band. Like, to do gigs. We'll bring Lucky in. He's up for it. He'll play bass."

Andy's face fell. And they'd get Carl Simmons to play guitar. Carl – cool hair, cool clothes. He looked like he should be fronting a band. Good bloke too. And Carl wasn't stuck in a wheelchair.

"Carl on guitar then?" Andy asked.

"Carl?" Daz said at once, "Yo' talking nonsense, bruv. We want the best."

"You bet, man," said Tess. "How could we do it without you?"

Well, that's nice, Andy thought.

"Cheers," he said. "But it's the wheelchair. I'll hold you back. You'll get narky with me, and then we'll fall out. It just won't work."

The others tried hard but they couldn't change Andy's mind.

Chapter 2
The Name

"What's up with you?" Sue said at breakfast. "Did something happen last night? I thought you'd still be rocking when I came in."

Andy chewed a weetabix and looked at his feet.

"I know," Sue said. "It was bound to happen. You've ... fallen in love with Tess, and then found out she's married. Or ... she's made a vow to be a nun. That's it, isn't it?"

Andy's mum was always teasing him. She teased everyone. She teased his dad when he was still at home.

"It's not fair," Andy said. "Why did it have to happen to us?"

Sue stopped smiling. They'd talked this over before. Many times.

"One bad moment on a wet road and a dark night," Andy moaned. "I get mashed up. Dad can't live with himself and pushes off. All our lives in ruins. How come the bloke in the other car gets away with it, and we have to put up with this?"

"I know," Sue said. "I know."

"However good I get on the guitar, what does it matter? Who's gonna care?"

He told his mum about the band.

Sue looked at him. She gave a sigh.

"It does matter. And you shouldn't turn them down."

"Yeah, right."

She took Andy's hands in hers.

"They're not doing it to be kind to you, love. You're very, very good. And you're more likely to lose your mates by saying no all the time. Andrew, are you listening to me?"

At the end of afternoon school, Andy found the others.

"Count me in," he said, looking sheepish. "If you'll still have me ..."

"Man, that rocks!" said Matt.

"Nice one," nodded Tess.

"Cool," agreed Lucky.

Daz whizzed Andy round in his wheelchair. "New song," he chanted. "We are the best. There's nothing we can't do ..."

"We'll be the greatest band in ..."

"... in Eastfield ..."

"... in the world ..."

"... in the universe ..."

"Just listen to us," said Andy. "What a bunch of bigheads ..."

"Wow," said Matt. "That's a good idea."

"What?" asked Daz.

"Bighead!" the others all shouted at once. As a name for the band, it just seemed to work.

"Now all we need is a gig," said Tess.

Chapter 3
The Gig

Mr Trent the music teacher was so excited, he hopped around on one leg.

"Great," he said. "I've been waiting for something like this. Let's have a lunch-time gig every month in the school hall. OK?"

"Cool," said Bighead.

"How about Wednesday in two weeks time? Are you up for that?"

"You bet!" said Bighead. And then they started to worry.

"What are we going to play? We haven't got that many songs."

"What are we going to wear? I'm not standing up there in my school uniform!"

"My bass needs mending."

"My kick drum pedal's bust."

"I've got a cold coming. My voice sounds Emo, man," wailed Tess.

"Your voice always sounds Emo, Tess!" Matt grinned.

Most days they practised in Eastfield's music room after school. Sometimes Carl came and hung out.

"You sound great," he said, but he looked sad. Andy began to feel bad about him. Two guitarists, and just one of them in the band.

****

When they came off stage after the gig, they were buzzing.

"We rocked," said Lucky.

"Didn't we just!" said Tess.

"How did it go?" Sue asked Andy later.

"Good!" said Andy. "Wish you could have been there. Maybe next time. You should have heard Tess sing!"

18

But soon Bighead started to find out that
not everyone thought like they did. And
they began to wonder if there'd be a 'next
time'.

"A bit rubbish," they heard someone say.

His friend agreed. "Boring, man!"

"Bighead! They got the name right!"

"Erm ... they won't be playing
Glastonbury just yet."

"A guitarist in a wheelchair? What's that
all about?"

Mr Fish, the science teacher, wasn't impressed either. "You'd do better to put more effort into your homework, Andy," he growled. "And stop wasting your time making that awful noise."

Ouch! But then, Mr Fish was about a hundred years old.

Bighead held a meeting. "What are we going to do?" they asked each other.

"It's me," said Andy sadly. "I told you!"

"It is so much not you," the rest of the band replied. "Shut up, Andy!"

Chapter 4
Advice

Bighead went back to see Mr Trent.

"We need advice," they said.

"OK," he said, "Are you sure you can handle it?"

"Go on," said Daz. "We can take it."

"OK then. Well, you weren't very slick,"
Mr Trent went on. "And there were too
many slow songs. And it is hard for Andy.
One moment he's playing rhythm, the next
lead – and all from that chair. Now, if you
had a second guitarist ..."

"Like Carl ..." said Andy.

"... Like Carl ... there'd be more movement on stage and Andy would have time to think. Andy, how about going wireless? Then there'd be no danger of catching yourself in your guitar lead. You can borrow my wireless rig, if you're careful."

"You ... play electric guitar, sir?" Andy asked, shocked.

"You mean you haven't heard of 'Tony Trent and the Night-Timers'?" Mr Trent smiled. "You haven't lived. Best blues band in ... well ... in Eastfield."

****

Carl was over the moon. "Great," he said. "I know most of the songs anyway. When's the next gig?"

"Try the Hill Park Hotel," said Mr Trent. "Ask for Toastie Black. He's the big man up there."

Chapter 5
Toastie

Toastie Black was a very big man. Under a greasy T-shirt, a huge belly fell out over the waist-band of his trousers. Just too many toasties!

"We could find you a spot," he said, "If you're any good. Are you any good?"

"We're very good," said Andy. "Ask Mr Trent."

"I did," replied Toastie. "And he said two things. He was right about the first."

"What was that?" asked Tess.

"He said you had attitude. So maybe he was right about the second."

"What was that?"

"He said you played OK. But I never take anything on trust. I wanna see for myself."

"Like test us out before we play?"

"You got it."

So a few days later there they were playing for Toastie. Carl had fitted in well. He was playing a lot of rhythm guitar and leaving the solos to Andy. Andy's wireless guitar system worked like a dream. He could move more freely, holding his guitar in the crook of one arm. With the other hand he worked the controls on the wheelchair.

Toastie sat on a chair at the back of the school hall, watching them. When they'd finished, he wobbled down towards them.

"I like it," he said. "But ..."

Bighead looked at him.

"The stage at Hill Park. It's tiny! With the wheelchair and that, my insurers would never agree to it. If anything went wrong – they'd have Toastie on toast. Sorry folks, no can do."

He spread his hands and looked at Andy with regret.

"Sorry, son," he said, "I thought you were like, their manager. Maybe ... if you sat it out, this one time ... after all, who needs two guitar players?"

"No way," said Bighead. "Forget it."

"He's well out of order. Just because Andy's in a wheelchair," Bighead raged at Mr Trent. "Let's sue."

"Don't be silly," said Andy.

"I am surprised," said Mr Trent. "Most of the time Toastie's better than that. We'll just have to think up something else."

The next day, Mr Trent found Andy. "How would Bighead fancy supporting The Night-Timers?" he asked. "Next weekend. Charity do at the Kingsmead Centre. Our support act has pulled out. Big stage. No worries about the insurance. What do you think?"

"Cool," said Andy.

"Now," said Mr Trent, "I've had another idea ..."

Chapter 6
Out of Control

Next Saturday morning, at Andy's house, Mr Trent was looking at Andy's wheelchair.

"The thing is," he was saying to Sue, "We've been looking at this the wrong way round. Andy's wheelchair isn't going to get in the way. It's what makes Bighead special."

"So let's put him up front and centre."

"And how are you going to do that?" she asked.

"Radio control."

"Radio control?"

"Why not? You play, Andy. I'll make you move. Like a model plane. Sort of." Mr Trent smiled.

"I'm not sure I like the sound of that," said Sue.

"Let's give it a go!" said Andy.

****

They tried it out a few times on their own in the school hall. Andy played and a few metres away Mr Trent pushed buttons on a remote control. Andy hoped Mr Trent knew what he was doing.

Daz and Lucky watched from the end of the hall.

"Mr Trent's lost it," Daz said. "It's mad."

"I like it," said Lucky. "It looks ... different."

"It sure does," Daz agreed.

Suddenly Andy leaned one way, the chair went the other, and the chair tipped. The guitar slipped from Andy's hands. He tried to grab it, missed and fell out of the chair. The guitar and Andy arrived on the hall floor at about the same time. One bang. One thud.

"Oh, no," said Daz, and he and Lucky
rushed up the hall.

There was no real damage. The guitar
had a small dent on its back and Andy had a
large bruise on his arm. Mr Trent looked
around in a nervous way.

"Wow," said Andy. "Rock and roll!"

****

"He's OK," Mr Trent said to Sue later on. "But no joking now, are you both happy with this?"

"It's up to Andy," Sue said. "But I think ... what's the point of living if you never take risks?"

"I go with that," said Andy.

"I miss singing so much," said Sue suddenly. "Andy should take every chance he's offered."

She looked a bit sad.

"Oh," said Mr Trent. "I didn't know you sang ..."

Chapter 7
Let's Hear It For Bighead

The Kingsmead Centre was packed.

"I'm wetting myself," said Matt. Andy could see he was shaking.

"Maybe Mr Trent could work your controls too," he said. "Then we might play more in time."

"Ha-ha," replied Matt. "No diving into the mosh pit tonight, wonder boy!"

There were a lot of people there, but you could have heard a spider sneeze as Bighead went on stage.

"Hello, Kingsmead, are you ready to rock?" Tess yelled.

Not a sound from the people in the hall. This was going to be hard going.

Bighead played their first number. Just a spatter of handclaps, plus a bit of muttering.

"Are you having a good time?" Tess shouted.

"Get on with it," yelled someone in the front row. Tess looked and shook her head at Andy. Andy shrugged his shoulders. Lucky stared at his feet. Daz fiddled with his keyboard.

"Right," shouted Matt from behind the drum kit. "I'm not having this. Let's show 'em!"

And they did. Tess sang her socks off. Matt hit the drums like he'd gone mad. Carl rocked out like he'd never rocked out before.

And slowly but surely, the people out there started loving them. Andy ripped out his solos, and the crowd whooped and cheered as he twisted and turned under the lights.

Tess's eyes were shining when at last they came off stage.

"Let's hear it for Bighead," Mr Trent shouted. The crowd were still going bonkers.

Tony Trent and The Night-Timers were good too, if you liked that sort of thing. Andy could see his mum. She was watching Tony Trent very closely as he played, with a strange little smile on her face.

After that, they had their photos taken for the local paper. A man with a pony-tail was talking to Mr Trent.

"Bighead, let me introduce you to Jack Jordan," Mr Trent said. "He's from Midland TV."

"The Battle of the Bands Show?" said Jack
Jordan. "You must have heard of it. Would
Bighead like a spot?"

Chapter 8
On the Box

"TV's cool," said Lucky, as they sat in Midland TV's dressing room drinking free lemonade and eating free sandwiches.

"I'm wetting myself," said Matt.

"Oh, shut up," shouted the rest of Bighead.

"Break a leg," Sue said to Andy. The rest of the band looked at her oddly. Andy grinned. It was a family joke.

Mr Trent was hopping about all over the place. He was very excited.

There were four bands, and each had to play two numbers. Bighead were on last. SALTFISH were a very good reggae act. TWELVE BARS played rock and roll. Badly. And ANGELS OF DOOM ground out six minutes of nasty trash-metal.

"Let's do it," said the floor manager, and suddenly Bighead were on the studio floor. Lights, cameras ... action!

They had fifteen minutes to sound-check and rehearse, and then before they knew it, the red light was on. Bighead were recording.

When they'd finished, they waited for the results.

"It doesn't matter," said Tess. "It was good fun."

"I don't care if we've won," said Lucky. "Not much."

"Yeah, right!" said Andy.

They watched in silence as Jack Jordan began to speak to camera.

"And the winners of this week's heat, who'll now go forward to the national show, Search for a Star, are ..."

Bighead held their breath.

... "SALTFISH".

Lucky looked depressed. Tess had a little cry.

Chapter 9
What Really Matters

"I'm so sorry, love," said Sue, as she drove Andy home.

"Well, I wanted us to win," said Andy. "And I thought we were the best. But when it comes to it, I don't care about Search for a Star."

"Don't you? If it was me, I would."

"It's the music that matters. And the people. How would being a star on TV change anything for the better?"

"You're amazing," said Sue. "But you're right, of course."

There was silence while they stared at the road in front for a bit.

"Talking of people, your Mr Trent's very nice," Sue said.

"Oh ...?"

"He said would I like to sing a few songs with the Night-Timers ..."

"And will you?"

"You said it. It's the music that counts."

"And people," said Andy.

"And people ..."

Andy looked across at his mum. She was smiling that odd little smile again. In fact, she looked much happier than she'd done in a while.

Andy found he was smiling too.

Dan is ill in bed.

"Can I get up, Mum?"

4

"No, Dan!"

5

Bill gets Dan
a can of pop.

7

But the can has gas in it.

8

The top pops up!

Dan is in a mess and his bed is in a mess.

10

11

"Can I get up, Mum?"

"No, Dan!"

13

Bill and Nell sit
on the bed.

But it dips and sags ...

... and tips up!

16

17

"Can I get up, Mum?"

"Yes, Dan. Get up!"

19

20

21

Puzzle Time!

Match the words that rhyme
to the pictures!

Bill

hill

well

sum

can

Mum

fell

gum

Nell

hum

bell

mill

man

fill

fan

Dan

See page 2 for answers!

Notes for parents and teachers

READING CORNER PHONICS has been structured to provide maximum support for children learning to read through synthetic phonics. The stories are designed for independent reading but may also be used by adults for sharing with young children.

The teaching of early reading through synthetic phonics focuses on the 44 sounds in the English language, and how these sounds correspond to their written form in the 26 letters of the alphabet. Carefully controlled vocabulary makes these books accessible for children at different stages of phonics teaching, progressing from simple CVC (consonant-vowel-consonant) words such as "top" (t-o-p) to trisyllabic words such as "messenger" (mess-en-ger). READING CORNER PHONICS allows children to read words in context, and also provides visual clues and repetition to further support their reading. These books will help develop the all important confidence in the new reader, and encourage a love of reading that will last a lifetime!

If you are reading this book with a child, here are a few tips:

1. Talk about the story before you start reading. Look at the cover and the title. What might the story be about? Why might the child like it?

2. Encourage the child to reread the story, and to retell the story in their own words, using the illustrations to remind them what has happened.

3. Discuss the story and see if the child can relate it to their own experience, or perhaps compare it to another story they know.

4. Give praise! Small mistakes need not always be corrected. If a child is stuck on a word, ask them to try and sound it out and then blend it together again, or model this yourself. For example "wish" w-i-sh "wish".

READING CORNER PHONICS covers two grades of synthetic phonics teaching, with three levels at each grade. Each level has a certain number of words per story, indicated by the number of bars on the spine of the book:

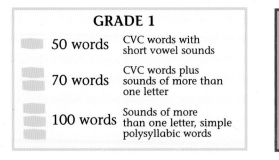

GRADE 1

	50 words	CVC words with short vowel sounds
	70 words	CVC words plus sounds of more than one letter
	100 words	Sounds of more than one letter, simple polysyllabic words

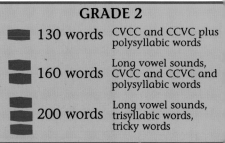

GRADE 2

	130 words	CVCC and CCVC plus polysyllabic words
	160 words	Long vowel sounds, CVCC and CCVC and polysyllabic words
	200 words	Long vowel sounds, trisyllabic words, tricky words